Brooklynn the Disobedient Unicorn

Alvin Walker

ISBN: 978-1-7378051-3-7 (Digital online)
ISBN: 978-1-7378051-4-4 (Paperback)
ISBN: 978-1-7378051-5-1 (Hardcover)

Library of Congress Control Number: In Public Data
Walker, Alvin

Any references to historical events, real people, or real places are used fictitiously. Names, characters, and places are products of the author's imagination.

Front cover image by Ayan Mansoori
Images by Ayan Mansoori

Printed in the United States of America.

First printing edition 2021.

Published by Alvin Walker
Contact Info: Bigidea62@gmail.com
www.amazon.com/author/alvinwalker.com

My Book

My Name: _____

My Address _____

My Phone Number _____

Dedication

I composed this book from the heart for my little granddaughter. She is three, and the world is a big place with so many things to discover.

Love you, Brooklynn,

Papaw

Table of Content

About the Author

Hello, my name is Alvin Walker. I am a sixty-three-year-old retiree who enjoys spending time with his grandkids. They are a joy to be around. I enjoy watching them grow up and learning new things. To see the wonder in their eyes when they discover something new in the world. The way they imitate the adults around them, so be a good example around your kids.

Introduction

This is about a young unicorn named Brooklynn who goes through so much trouble by disobeying her parents. Brooklynn soon finds out that there are results to her actions.

Chapter 1
Brooklynn becomes lost in the Forest

Brooklynn's parent warns her repeatedly not to wander away from them, but she never listens. One day Brooklynn and her parents were walking in the wood. Brooklynn wandered off and became lost. She was very scared, and it took hours to find her.

Chapter 2
Brooklynn Does Not Like to Get Her Hair Combed

Brooklynn argues with her mother when she combs her hair.

She cries and screams at the top of her voice.

Chapter 3
Brooklynn Does Not Want
to Take a Bath

Brooklynn's mom said it's time to take your bath. Brooklynn started crying and yelled, "Nooo!" and ran from her mother. Later, the other unicorns teased Brooklynn about her smell. This made Brooklynn think that she wouldn't be getting teased if she had taken a bath as her mother said.

Chapter 4
Brooklynn Never Cleans Up Her Room

Brooklynn's dad tells her to clean up her room, but Brooklynn makes so many excuses. She did not listen to her dad, and the room stayed messy. That night Brooklynn got up from sleeping to use the bathroom. The light was off, and Brooklynn tripped over the stuff on the floor. Brooklynn hurt her leg. If she had only cleaned her room up.

Chapter 5
Brooklynn Always Playing and Taking Others Stuff Without Asking

Brooklynn is always prowling around the house, picking up everyone's stuff without permission. Her mom and dad have talked to her about this, and she still does it. Yesterday, Brooklynn went through her mother's jewelry box and lost her mother's best diamond earrings. Her mother was upset about it. Brooklynn realized what she had done hurt her mother. Brooklynn loves her mom very much. She tells her mother she is deeply sorry and will not do it again.

Chapter 6
Brooklynn Always Being Mean to Her Friends

Brooklynn is always mean to her friends. When she is sleepy or "in her feeling," that is what her parents call it. She is always bossy and wants to be the leader. But her friends are tired of it and have stopped visiting. Brooklynn became sad. Brooklyn's mother had a long talk with her about treating her friend the way she wanted to be treated.

Chapter 7
Brooklynn Stays Up Too Late at Night

Brooklynn is up watching TV and eating late at night when everyone is asleep.

Then she ends up with a stomachache.

Chapter 8
Brooklynn Climb Up on the Cabinets

Brooklynn's parents had told her countless times not to climb up on the kitchen cabinets. One day she almost reached the top and grabbed the cabinet handle; it came loose and Brooklynn fell. Brooklynn hurt her foot. She did not climb anymore.

Chapter 9
Brooklynn Putting on Her Mother's Makeup

Brooklynn always gets into her mother's makeup and puts it all over her face. She also makes a big mess on the floor. Brooklynn gets the makeup in her eyes, and it hurts her.

Chapter 10
Brooklynn Loves to Write on the Walls

Brooklynn has an artist side to her. She loves to write on the walls with Crayola crayons or anything to write with. Brooklynn's mom and dad had to repaint the walls, which was expensive.

The Conclusion

Brooklynn soon learns that being disobedient to her parents can get her in trouble.

She realizes that Mom and Dad were only trying to protect her from hurting herself and others. They were trying to teach her to be responsible and organized.

"So, one day, I can take care of myself!" Brooklynn said.

The End

www.ingramcontent.com/pod-product-compliance
Lightning Source LLC
Chambersburg PA
CBHW041004170626
46815CB00002B/162